A LITTLE BOOK OF
Teddy bear tales

ILLUSTRATED BY
Juliette Clarke

HUTCHINSON
LONDON · MELBOURNE · AUCKLAND · JOHANNESBURG

Produced by Templar Publishing Ltd,
107 High Street, Dorking, Surrey RH4 1QA,
for Hutchinson Children's Books

First published 1987 by Hutchinson Children's Books
An imprint of Century Hutchinson Ltd,
Brookmount House, 62-65 Chandos Place, Covent Garden,
London WC2N 4NW

Century Hutchinson Group (Australia) Pty Ltd,
16-22 Church Street, Hawthorn, Melbourne, Victoria 3122

Century Hutchinson Group (NZ) Ltd,
32-34 View Road, PO Box 40-086, Glenfield, Auckland 10

Century Hutchinson Group (SA) Pty Ltd,
PO Box 337, Bergvlei 2012, South Africa

Set in Times Roman by Templar Type

British Library Cataloging in Publication Data

A Little book of teddy bear stories.
   1. Children's stories, English
   I. Clarke, Juliette
   823'.01'089282 [J]   PZ7

ISBN 0-09-171790-6

Colour separations by Positive Colour Ltd, Maldon, Essex
Printed and bound by L.E.G.O., Vincenza, Italy

Contents

George Bear's Birthday

by Jane Varley

t was George Bear's birthday. His friends, Mandy the doll, Big Florrie the dog and Elsie the elephant, had saved up to buy him an extra special present. They used twenty-six pieces of birthday paper to wrap it up.

It was such a huge present that they had to tie a rope to it and pull it to George's house. George was very excited. He ripped off the glossy wrapping paper and there stood a great big, shiny, blue, three-wheeled cycle.

"Oh, my," cried George, his mouth smiling right up to his ears. "A tricycle! Thank you, thank you, everyone."

"Come on then," said Big Florrie. "Let's see you ride it."

"It's big and strong, and you can carry lots of things in the baskets," said Elsie.

"And it won't tip over," added Mandy Doll. She was a very careful person.

"Old Bear might just manage to tip that

over," said Black Velvet Cat, who had come in to watch the fun – Cat always saw the dark side of things.

Bear clambered on to the seat of the tricycle and put his feet firmly on the pedals. How fine he looked! He rang the silver bell: Ting-a-ting! All his friends clapped their hands and jumped up and down with excitement. Except, that is, for Black Velvet Cat, who sat under the rose bush, with his tail tucked neatly around his paws, and looked smug.

"I bet he'll fall off before the end of the day," he muttered darkly.

"My friends," said Bear, "I have a wonderful idea. Let's all go down to the fields by the river and have a picnic."

Everyone helped to make the picnic. Soon the baskets of the tricycle were packed tight with all sorts of delicious things. There were ham, cheese-and-pickle and peanut-butter sandwiches, crisps and crackers, crunchy chocolate bars; bananas and grapes.

"Don't forget the drink and the cups," said Mandy Doll. She put three cartons of orange juice and three cartons of apple juice into the front basket.

"We're off!" shouted Bear, waving his hat in the air.

The road down the hill was steep. Bear pressed hard on the pedals. The more he pedalled, the faster the tricycle went. After only a few minutes Bear's friends had to run to keep up with him.

"Slow down," panted Mandy Doll. She was already out of breath from running.

"Wheeee!" yelled Bear, not listening, and he took his feet off the pedals.

"Oh no!" squealed Mandy Doll. "I can't look." She covered her eyes with her apron.

"Put on the brakes," shouted Elsie, in her loudest voice.

"What brakes?" came Bear's voice faintly, as he vanished around the corner at the bottom of the hill.

The friends looked at one another in horror. Then they raced down the hill after him. Round the corner at the bottom, they saw the shiny blue tricycle. It lay on its side, with one wheel spinning. Picnic food and cartons of drink were scattered all over the road. But where was George Bear?

Just then, there was a great sneeze from the middle of a bush. It was Bear!

"Are you all right?" fussed Mandy Doll, brushing grass and leaves out of Bear's fur.

"Perfectly!" said Bear. "It wasn't prickly."

"It might be next time," said Black Cat, darkly.

"But what about my beautiful tricycle?" howled Bear. "And our picnic. Look, the food is all over the road!"

"I expect it's all right," said Big Florrie. "Come on everyone! Help me pick everything up."

And so they did. Luckily, none of the food was spoilt and the cartons of drink were only a little bit dented. Bear wheeled the tricycle into the field and they laid out their picnic in a grassy spot under the trees.

Everyone ate masses and masses of food, but Bear ate the most. When it was time to go home his friends helped him onto his tricycle. But Bear had eaten so much he couldn't pedal up the hill. His tummy got in the way of his knees.

"I know," cried Elsie. "Someone run up to Bear's house and get that piece of rope. We'll tie the rope to the handlebars of the tricycle. Then, if we all pull together, we'll be able to haul old Bear up to the top of the hill."

And so, huffing and puffing, that is what they did. Even Black Cat helped.

Simon and the Toyshop

by Sally Sheringham

imon Teddy Bear was the oldest toy in Mrs Grant's toy shop. He loved living there, and the other toys loved him being there, too. They called him the 'life and soul of the toy shop'.

The reason why Simon had managed to stay there for so long was that no one ever wanted to buy him. And that was because of Simon's special plan.

Whenever a likely-looking customer came into the shop, Simon would undo the bow around his neck to make himself look untidy. Next he would hang his head on one side and squint. If that didn't seem to put the customer off, Simon would stick out his tongue. And if that didn't work, he would fall over on the shelf. If the customer tried to pick him up Simon would punch them with his paw.

Simon's plan had always worked very well. No girl or boy wanted a squinting, untidy, bad-tempered teddy bear to cuddle.

"Why should anyone want to be sold and risk ending up forgotten in some cupboard, or chewed to pieces by a pet dog?" Simon would often remark to any toy who cared to listen. "We're much more comfortable here, among friends!" And when any toy was sold, Simon would always shout, "Bad luck!"

Now Simon would never admit it to the other toys, but every now and again he did wish that he had someone to love and cuddle him, especially at night. For nights at the toy shop could be long and lonely, and the shelf was very hard.

Then one morning, a little girl and her mother came into the toy shop. While the mother talked to Mrs Grant, the little girl came over to look at the bears. She glanced at all the other toys but when she came to Simon, she stopped and stared. Simon scowled and squinted back.

Then he stuck out his tongue. But the little girl didn't seem to mind at all, and she picked him up to cuddle him. Simon punched her, but only gently, because even he had to admit she seemed quite a nice little girl.

"Mummy, this is the one I want, please," said the little girl, holding up Simon.

The toys all gasped. Surely she didn't want to buy *Simon*? The little girl's mother looked at Simon and wrinkled up her nose.

"He's not a very handsome bear," she said. "Are you sure he's the one you want, Sarah?"

"Oh, that old rogue!" laughed Mrs Grant, when Sarah's mother asked for Simon. "You can have him for half price."

"Bad luck, Simon," cried the toys, as he was carried, still scowling and squinting, out of the shop. They all felt very sad. The shop wouldn't be the same without him.

"Half price, indeed," muttered Simon, as Sarah got into the car with him.

When they arrived at Simon's new home, Sarah dressed him in a smart green jacket and took him out for a long ride on her bicycle. Simon found that he was enjoying himself so much that he had quite forgotten to scowl and squint. He liked being cuddled, too. In fact, he settled down in his new home surprisingly quickly. But he still missed all his friends in the toy shop.

One day he overheard Sarah's mother talking to her. "I start work at Mrs Grant's toy shop tomorrow," she said. "You can come too, if you like. Mrs Grant said you could."

Simon's ears pricked up.

"And you must come too, Simon," said Sarah to him. "Then you'll be able to say hello to your friends. That's why we got you for half price," she added, "because Mummy is going to work for Mrs Grant."

How thrilled the toys were to see Simon again! And how he had changed in the short time he had been away – there wasn't a scowl, or a squint to be seen! Simon was delighted to be back to being the life and soul of the toy shop, but he was happy to have a proper home to go to at night, with a warm bed and a friendly arm around him.

"It's what's known as having the best of both worlds," said Simon happily to any toy who cared to listen.

Toy's World

by Stanley Bates

t was August Bank Holiday and Mr and Mrs Brown, Simon and Vicky had all gone out for the day. The house was empty, apart from Mog the cat, fast asleep in her basket – or was it? Upstairs, in the playroom, something very strange was happening!

Very slowly, the lid of the toy box opened. First one paw appeared, then another, and then a face peeped out – it was Teddy! He carefully looked around the room, then he said,

"It's all clear, come on everybody. Time for our own holiday outing!"

One by one the toys climbed out of the toy box, while Teddy held the lid open.

"Excuse me Teddy," said a very small voice right at the bottom. "I don't think I'll be able to climb out of the toy box."

"Of course you will, Tiny Doll. I'll help," said Teddy, and he lifted her up and put her on the edge of the box.

"Now then, Fire Engine," shouted Teddy. "Put your ladder up to where Tiny Doll is standing, and she can climb down."

"Oh, thank you Teddy. I'll go and make us all some tea," she cried. And she ran into the dolls' house, slamming the door behind her.

"Now remember, they will be back at tea-time. Until then, I'm in charge," said Teddy.

"Yes, Sir!" shouted all the toys.

"Good. Now go and enjoy yourselves," he laughed.

Toy Soldier started marching up and down, and up and down, and Teddy took the salute. Then Toy Soldier spoke:

"All right if I go for a walk in the forest, Sir?"

"Certainly, Soldier," said Teddy.

And Toy Soldier went for a walk in the big, dark forest of green tassels dangling from the bedspread, which someone had thrown over the back of a chair.

Panda called after him, "Don't be too long. I think it's going to rain – there's a huge cloud in the sky!" He was looking up at the great, grey duvet hanging over the edge of the bed.

"Where has the train got to?" Teddy asked. "I can hear his whistle, but I can't see him." He bent down and looked under the chest of drawers.

"Sorry Teddy, I'm stuck in this tunnel. There's something on the line." Train was getting very steamed up. Teddy reached for the torch, and shone it under the chest of drawers.

"Don't worry, Train, there's a fallen tree on the line. I'll soon remove it." He put the torch down, picked up a pencil, and pushed a green feather duster off the track.

"Thanks," said Train. "I'll soon make up lost time." And away he went.

Nurse was standing by an empty shoe box.

"Everyone's out enjoying themselves today, Teddy – look, my hospital's empty."

Just then, Teddy heard a whining sound. It was Puppy Dog. He was sitting down, looking at a large bean bag in the corner of the room. "Woof! Woof! I'll never be able to climb that mountain."

"Well, try again another time," said Teddy, as he patted Puppy Dog.

Then Teddy remembered a new toy had arrived that day. It was in a square box, with a small catch on one side. Teddy pushed the catch over. The lid flew off and a Jack-in-the-Box leapt out, laughing.

"Ha! ha! ha! That gave you a surprise – I'm Jack-in-the-Box – nice to meet you all," and he swayed from side to side.

Then Rocking Horse gave a loud "Neigh-hey-hey! I'm off to the races." He started rocking backwards and forwards, backwards and forwards, backwards and forwards. Teddy got quite dizzy watching him.

The door of the dolls' house opened, and Tiny Doll called out, "Tea-time," in a very small voice that no one could hear. So Teddy called out in his big voice, "Tea-time!"

Everyone heard Teddy, and they all rushed into the dolls' house to have tea.

Just at that moment, the family came home. Simon and Vicky raced upstairs to play. They looked inside the toy box – but it was empty!

"That's funny," they said. "We left all the toys in here."

But when they looked inside the dolls' house, there were all the toys. And, do you know, they looked just as if they were having tea!

Growler and the Polar Bears

by Jane Garrett

rowler tried hard to look fierce, but his fat, furry face made this difficult. He hated being a cuddly teddy. He wanted to be a big, bad bear. He practised sounding gruff and tough. It was Tommy's daddy who first called him Growler, and the name stuck.

Growler longed to escape from Tommy's warm, untidy bedroom and go off and live with *real* bears.

"I'll show them," he growled. "Teddy, indeed!"

Tommy and his daddy had been talking all evening about the zoo. They were planning to visit it next day. Growler heard the word "bears" and pricked up his ears. Bears! Real bears! He *had* to find a way inside that zoo.

"Growler's all cuddly today," said Tommy, rather surprised, next morning. "Can I take him, too?"

"Yes," said daddy. "But don't lose him."

Tommy tucked Growler under his arm and marched off to the car.

"Take care you don't drop him," shouted his mother.

Once they were safely through the green iron turnstile into the zoo, Growler could hardly keep still for excitement. There were signs everywhere. They pointed to elephants, crocodiles, lions, giraffes – but where were the bears?

"Ah! There they are," sighed Growler with relief, spotting the bear sign. But, oh dear, he was being taken away in quite the wrong direction – towards a dolphin show instead.

It was now or never! Growler gave a quick wriggle and fell on to the path. Tommy never even noticed. Now to find those bears!

He was so excited when he caught sight of another sign post pointing to a bear enclosure that he never stopped to see what *kind* of bears they were. Trotting around the corner, Growler took one look and caught his breath in amazement. They were enormous, shaggy, creamy-white Polar Bears!

Growler was so impressed at how wonderful the bears were that he rushed forward, shouting, "Hello, it's me. I'm a bear! How do you do? I'm *so* glad I've found you ..." He just couldn't stop talking.

The Polar Bears looked down in amazement at this short, fat, furry creature with stumpy legs.

"*Who* are *you*?" boomed the biggest one, reaching down with his long, thin, elegant nose and sniffing Growler. "Oho! Man smell," he murmured. "So where have *you* come from, little man-friend bear?"

"I've escaped!" cried Growler. "I don't want to live in Tommy's bedroom. I'm a bear and I want to live like a bear. Please can I stay with you?"

The other bears crowded round. "They're terribly big," thought Growler suddenly. "I hope they aren't the *very* fierce kind of bears that would just step on a little growly bear like me." He began to feel nervous.

"You'd probably like to have a wash," said one of the bears. "Come for a dip in the lovely cold water."

"But I'd get all wet and soggy," cried Growler, alarmed. "I'd sink..." The bears looked very surprised.

"You must be hungry after your escape," said another one, kindly. "I was saving this fish for later, but you can have it now, if you like." And he pushed a shining silver mackerel towards Growler.

Growler didn't know *what* to do. He couldn't possibly eat a whole fish – but what would happen if the bears got angry! Suddenly there was a loud clanging of gates and chains. The bears stopped staring at Growler and swung around. The zoo keepers were doing their evening round.

"Hello," said the keeper, smiling down at Growler. "However did *you* get in here? Shoo, you lot!" As the Polar Bears moved away from

Growler, the keeper unlocked the gate, slipped inside and picked him up. "You must be the missing teddy bear! Your Tommy will be glad to know you're safe and sound."

Deep down in the safety of the keeper's pocket, Growler thought and thought. Icy water and cold raw fish – that was no life for a bear like him. He missed Tommy's cosy bed-room, with the warmth of the radiator by the window, and the patchwork quilt on Tommy's bed. Oh, he did so want to go home!

Next day, Tommy snatched Growler with a shout of joy from the Lost Property basket, where he had spent an uncomfortable night sandwiched between a broken umbrella and a bag of knitting.

How happy Growler was to be home again! He never told anyone about his Polar Bear adventure – and he never, ever growled fiercely at Tommy again.

Buzz, the Little Bear

by Gina Stewart

Buzz was a very small bear, not more than two inches high and Julie, who had bought him with her own pocket money, loved him a lot.

"You're a *great* little bear", she would tell him, "and I'll look after you for ever and ever."

Buzz was such a small bear that he fitted easily into the pocket of Julie's school shirt, and he got used to sitting there quietly during lessons, peering over the edge and watching everything that went on.

At night, Julie carefully took Buzz out of her pocket and put him in his little bed in the dolls' house, where he had a number of equally small friends. And at weekends when she rode her bicycle on the common, Julie would tuck Buzz into the belt of her jeans, or the front of her dungarees, and would take him with her wherever she went.

One day, when Julie was out riding her bicycle, she dropped Buzz into a puddle, and

when she picked him up the little bear was so muddy you could hardly see him at all.

"Poor Buzz!" she said. "I'd better not drop you again." And she pushed him deep into the pocket of her jeans.

"Right," said her mother when she arrived back home. "Off with those muddy clothes."

Julie, who had quite forgotten that Buzz was still in the pocket of her jeans, did as her mother asked. She changed into warm, clean clothes and sat down to have her tea.

Meanwhile, something terrible was happening to Buzz. He felt himself being bundled up. Then he was shoved into somewhere dark and noisy. Woosh! Water suddenly poured in. Try as he might, he could not move. Each time he was about to stand up – Wheee! he was knocked flat and whizzed round and round. First it was hot water, then it was cold water, and there was a dreadful taste of soap in his mouth. Just as he got used to spinning in one direction, everything stopped and he started to spin in the other direction. Five times, Buzz felt all the hot water drain away and hoped that this was the end of his troubles. Five times, fresh, cold water rinsed over him again. Finally, there was one tremendously long and dizzying spin. Then there was wonderful stillness.

Buzz was still deep inside the pocket of Julie's jeans and couldn't see what was going on. He felt himself being pulled about and shaken a little and then pushed somewhere else.

"Oh, no!" he cried, as the spinning started again. "Not more cold water!"

This time what he felt was not cold water, but warm air. The air blew Buzz out of the pocket and soon he was lying comfortably among a bundle of clothes, being gently tumbled this way and that. Through the window of the dryer he could see into the kitchen, where Julie was having her tea.

"Oh, no! It's Buzz!" exclaimed Julie, when she saw her favourite bear pressed against the glass of the tumble-dryer, going round and round and round. She opened the door and rescued him.

"Just look at yourself," she laughed. "You're all fluffy!"

And it must be said, Buzz did look very soft and smell very nice after his ordeal. But Julie decided not to risk this sort of thing happening again. From that day on, he stayed safely in the dolls' house. The new, fluffy Buzz was the envy of all his friends!